To the
RESCUE!

For Maggie Byer-Sprinzeles
and her heroic crew:
Mike, Max & Paul-C.S.

LITTLE SIMON
An imprint of Simon & Schuster Children's Publishing Division
1230 Avenue of the Americas, New York, New York 10020
Copyright © 2003 Mattel, Inc.
All rights reserved.
MATCHBOX™, MATCHBOX logo, and MATCHBOX HERO CITY™
and logo are trademarks owned by and used under license from Mattel, Inc.
All rights reserved.
READY-TO-READ, LITTLE SIMON, and colophon are
registered trademarks of Simon & Schuster. All rights reserved,
including the right of reproduction in whole or in part in any form.
Manufactured in the United States of America
First Edition
2   4   6   8   10   9   7   5   3   1
The Library of Congress has cataloged the library edition as follows:
Library Edition ISBN 0-689-86148-6
Paperback ISBN 0-689-85898-1
Schoberle, Cecile.
Matchbox : to the rescue! / by Cecile Schoberle ; illustrations by
Isidre Mones and Marc Mones.-- 1st ed.
p. cm. -- (Ready-to-read)
Summary: Rhyming verses describe a variety of
rescue vehicles and the work that they do.
ISBN 0-689-85898-1 (alk. paper) -- ISBN 0-689-86148-6 (Library Edition)
[1. Emergency vehicles--Fiction. 2. Rescue work--Fiction. 3. Stories in rhyme.]
I. Mones, Isidre, ill. II. Mones, Marc, ill. III. Title. IV. Series.
PZ8.3.S29733Mat 2003
[E] --dc21
2003005579

To the RESCUE!

By Cecile Schoberle
Illustrations by Isidre Mones,
Marc Mones, and Ivan & Moxo

Ready-to-Read

Little Simon

New York   London   Toronto   Sydney   Singapore

To the rescue!

To the rescue!

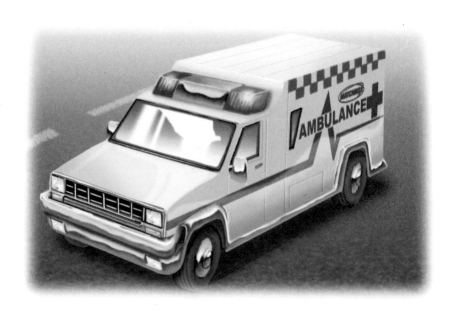

Help is coming

for you and me.

A chief's car drives fast.

It races past.

A siren wails on top.

The fire chief yells,

"Please stand back!"

His car comes to a stop.

An engine roars.

A bell *clang-clangs*.

A ladder is raised high.

Fire truck hoses
spray the house.
"Saved!" the family cries.

"Move the truck,"
   the fire chief calls.
"We have another job now."
   He gets in the bucket.
   It cranks up in the tree.
   The kitten says, "Meow!"

A tanker signals.

There is trouble.

A fire boat gets the alarm.

The fire boat
puts out the fire.
It saves the tanker ship
from harm.

Police cars zoom
over the hill.
Someone robbed the bank!

Red lights flash.

The robber is caught.

The banker says, "Thanks!"

A police boat

has a special radio

and carries safety floats.

It splashes through
the waves.

It helps the other boats.

A lady is stuck!

There is a flood.

Is there any hope?

A helicopter flies low.

There she is!

Police drop down a rope.

Waaarrgghh!

goes an ambulance siren.

Cars pull aside.

The ambulance rushes
to a hospital.
What a fast ride!

A digger is stuck!

But this tow truck is tough.

It can pull the digger along!

"Just in time!"

the workers call.

"We needed

something strong."

The snow is deep.

A skier is lost.

He does not know

what to do.

A helicopter searches.

The crew yells out,

"Grab on, we've got you!"

People get sick
or lost or hurt.

See how fast the rescue
vehicles go.

To the rescue!

To the rescue!

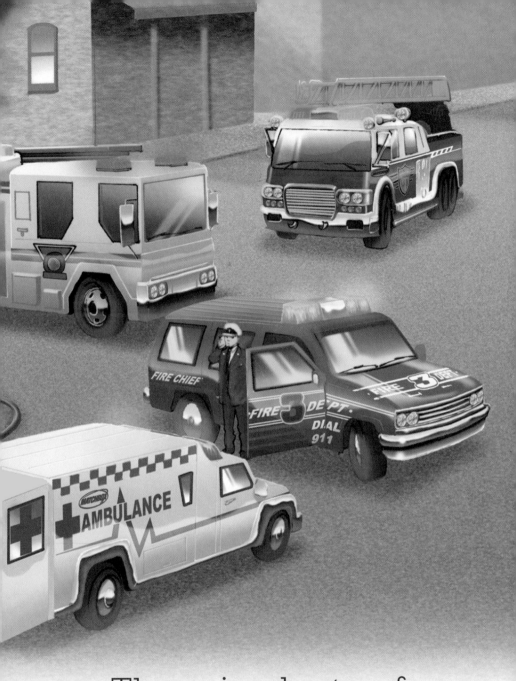

There is plenty of

help around.